Cyril Kwashie

A Migrant Fisherman in
Ghana, West Africa

Cyril Kwashie

A Migrant Fisherman in Ghana, West Africa

Written by:

Louvenia Jenkins

Foreword

The story which follows is based on an actual account of one migrant fisherman, Cyril Kwashie, whom I met in the summer of 1970 when I visited Ghana, West Africa with a group of Southern California teachers from the University of Southern California*.

Cyril Kwashie's story is but one of many waiting to be told about migrant fishermen and their families. These people about whom this story is written moved from their homes in the southeastern part of Ghana, called the Volta Region, to the central part of Ghana in Cape Coast; some 300 miles away in 1936 to make a better life for themselves. Though life has not been easy for them, they have remained with the hope that their futures will be brighter.

*The group of more than twenty teachers, funded by the
United States Department of Education, traveled under the
sponsorship of the University of Southern California and the
University of California at Los Angeles. The educators
represented approximately seven school districts in the
southern region of California. They spent six weeks living
with families while gathering social science data in Senegal,
Ghana, and Nigeria.

Introduction

In Ghana, West Africa, where agriculture is the most widespread occupation, fishing is an important industry, occupying from over 70 percent of the entire working population. Most of the fish caught comes from the sea and includes many eating species, of which the sea bream is one. The most common catch, however, is herring. Fishing, as an industry, in Ghana has many problems. One major issue is the lack of proper refrigeration and transporting facilities from large cities to inland communities.

Previously most of the fishing had been done by fishermen who lived in villages by the sea. Usually, one man whose "Wealth" permitted him to own a boat and net is considered the head man.

Cyril O. K. Kwashie

Cyril O. K. Kwashie, a sturdily built man, stood proudly in the village courtyard awaiting his visitors. From where he stood, he could see Bozu, the man he trusted most in the village. Bozu was busily mending the net which Kwashie owned and which all the men in the village used when they set out on their daily fishing trips. If it were a good day when the men left at 7:30 a.m., their wives should not expect them until late evening. If the first casting of the net brought a few fish the fourteen men would agree that only one casting should be done that day. In this way, they saved the rest of the day for repairing their houses, farming their fields of cassava, yams, tomatoes, and peppers, and weaving mats, or idling away the time by talking, telling jokes or listening to some man's favorite story.

As Kwashie stood watching Bozu he remembered why he had left his home in the Volta Region of Southeastern Ghana, West Africa, as a young man some thirty years ago. While deep in thought he said out loud, "Why has life been unkind to me?" The pain of remembering his departure from the Volta Region made him groan a bit as if an old wound had been reopened.

He said in conversation to himself, "My hopes of doing something grand were dashed when I was told that fishing was the best career I could follow since I was not prepared to do anything else."

"How can one man make this decision. for another man," thought Kwashie.

"Every-man," continued Kwashie loudly to himself, "deserves a chance to prove his worth to himself first, and then to his fellow man."

Nevertheless, Kwashie had been anxious to be successful and he accepted the advice given to him. He reasoned, "I must make a quick decision. After all, I am now married. I have my wife Aku, and son Kofi, to care for. I want to care for them in a grand style." His career decided, Kwashie began fishing in the Volta Region.

After several months of attempting to fish, he said to Aku, "I cannot continue to fish here."

"Why?" questioned Aku.

"I cannot," Kwashie answered, "because competition with other fishermen makes it impossible to make sufficient money for us to live on and to save."

Aku questioned, "What are we to do?"

"We will move west to Cape Coast," said Kwashi "I have heard," he continued, "that fishing for herring is better there than here. I shall recruit some villagers to go with us."

Kwashie and His Settlement Move to Cape Coast

Soon after, his decision was made, Kwashie, his family and fifty other men with their families, agreed that their lives could be better along the coast, by leaving the Volta Region.

Upon arriving at Cape Coast there were decisions to be made, mainly about fishing, after the men had hastily built their houses.

"Men," Kwashie announced, "it appears that fishing is good here from October to April."

"Then, we shall work hard during those months," a man interrupted.

"We shall save our money," shouted another!

"And then what?" questioned Kwashie.

The first man that spoke said, "My name is Bozu. I suggest that during the months from October to April, when fishing is the best, we work hard. We will save our money for the time when we will return to the Volta Region to build our homes and stay permanently."

Meanwhile, during the rainy season from April to October, when fishing is not good, I suggest that we fish when conditions permit" Bozu continued. "When fishing is too poor, we should visit our homes in the Volta Region," added Bozu. Kwashie liked this fellow Bozu, He sounds wise, Kwashie thought to himself.

"Friend, Bozu," Kwashie hollered out, "what you have said is wise indeed. We shall follow your advice."

The group nodded in agreement.

So it was, Duakor Village Number 1, as this village was called, had its birth. As a result, the villagers began their new life in harmony and of one purpose.

Kwashie Recalls His Visits by the Regional Commissioner of Cape Coast

It was on a bright sunny day in August, long after Kwashie, his family, and the other families of the fishing village had settled in Cape Coast, that he expected his California guests. The day before, the sea had been rough.

"The men and I," Bozu began, "should wait a couple of days before going out to sea. Before we attempt to go, we will test the water to see if the moon will cause the sea to continue to be rough and dangerous."

Kwashie nodded his approval of Bozu's plan as he drifted off into thought. He shifted his weight a bit uneasily as he thought about the first time he set foot on the shore of Cape Coast in the central part of Ghana, West Africa.

"As I remember," he said out loud, "there was nothing in sight for yards around when my group arrived, put up our first houses and settled down to enjoy fishing off the coast."

Some years after they had arrived,

Kwashie recalled when the Regional Commissioner of Cape Coast visited, he asked Kwashie and his group to return to the Volta Region. "Why?" Kwashie had remembered asking.

As the Commissioner could give no reasons for the request Kwashie chose to disobey it.

He called the villagers together and said, "The Regional Commissioner from Cape Coast has asked us to leave this area."

"Why?" One man shouted, angrily.

"I asked the same question, friend, but he did not give an answer. I suppose," said Kwashie wearily, "it is because our village with its hastily built and temporary-looking houses is unsightly."

"Could it be that we too are unsightly and therefore unwanted," shouted an old toothless man.

"That is most likely part of the reason," answered Kwashie. "We shall not leave.

Instead, we shall move further inland," he continued.

It appeared that their departure had gone unnoticed and Kwashie and his men had settled down to enjoy their life of fishing.

The tranquility of the lives of the fishermen and their families was broken after they had been in their new location a year.

One morning very, very early someone shouted, 'Fire, fire! Run or you'll be burned to death!"

As Kwashie gathered his family and led them and the villagers from the inferno, he said, with anger, "Who did this? Who destroyed our village which we worked hard to build and maintain?"

The next day, Kwashie knew he had the answer, when the Regional Commissioner appeared. He looked past the Commissioner as the men attempted to sift from the rubble salvageable items.

With perspiration streaming down his brows, mingled with tears on his cheeks,

Kwashie could hardly believe his ears as he heard the Commissioner say to him and the villagers, "Return to your homes in the Volta Region! Cape Coast is not the place for you."

Kwashie was too shocked to speak but he again would disobey this unjust order.

Everyone left except Kwashie. He said to his wife, Aku, "I am more determined than ever to succeed. I shall succeed."

Instead of going to the Volta Region as he was instructed, Kwashie moved further inland to the village of Kowadu where he stayed happily for several years.

Kwashie's New Settlement- -Duakor Village Number 2

After the Coup D' Etat, when Nkrumah's regime ended, Kwashie and his family moved from Kowadu to his present site of Duakor Village Number 2. He was joined there by forty-two other countrymen, most of whom had been in his first settlement.

One bright warm morning long after the move, Kwashie said, to his wife Aku, as she hurried about in the open kitchen which formed part of the courtyard, "It appears that our old problems with the Commissioner are over."

Aku, who was not as optimistic as Kwashie, nodded and continued walking as she said, "I hope you are right, Cyril."

In this present site, in the beginning, when the fish had been plentiful, life had been easy. The villagers had saved enough money to take home to build fine new houses.

Later, as more and more fishermen using motorboats came and with the opening of a nearby dam, the supply of fish was diminishing. Many of Kwashie's good men started returning home.

As Kwashie thought of his new problem he flinched. "Where will I get the thirty or forty new men I need," he asked loudly enough for his wife, who was standing nearby, to hear.

Until this time Aku had been busily preparing the noonday meal in the kitchen which opened to the village courtyard. Monica, their eldest daughter, had just finished washing the breakfast dishes. She stood beside her mother and fanned the charcoal which fueled the burner over which her mother had placed a pot of groundnut soup.

"Monica," her mother called over her shoulder, "did you finish cleaning the fish?"

"Yes, Mother," Monica said cheerfully. "I have placed them on the racks over the big ovens to smoke. Do you not see them there?"

"Yes, my daughter, I do. You are a very obedient girl. Would you like to go to the market in Accra with me tomorrow and sell the fish?"

Monica responded eagerly, "Oh yes, Mother!"

She knew that going to the market was something that girls in the village were rarely permitted to do. She could hardly contain her enthusiasm.

"We shall start very early then, my child. Tell your younger sister, Frances, she is to sweep the kitchen in your place and to tend to Baby Kwami while we are away,"

"Yes, Mother," Monica shouted back as she went happily to find her younger sister Frances.

Bozu's Honesty in Question

Aku, by this time, had joined her husband in the main courtyard. She took this opportunity to remind him that if his trusted man Bozu kept better records of their fish sales their profit would possibly be more.

"What you do not understand," Kwashi pointed out, "is that it is not Bozu alone who keeps the records. I, too, record the sale of the fish. Our end-of-the-year records must agree," he emphasized.

Aku pressed her point of possible dishonesty by Bozu.

"Do you remember the day last week when you left the village and instructed Bozu to measure out the fish and give it to the women to prepare for a sale?" Kwashie nodded in agreement as Aku continued, "You further instructed him to caution the women to make sure their sales were recorded properly upon their return."

"Yes, I remember," Kwashie interrupted irritated, "what was unusual about it?"

Aku explained, "Bozu did not fill the measuring tins fully. Perhaps what was left would be his gain alone."

At this point, Kwashie's irritation with his wife could no longer be contained. He said, "I, Cyril Kwashie, am still the head man of this village. If dishonesty is proven I will not hesitate to ask the local authorities to deal with the man properly."

Aku knew by the sound of her husband's voice it was useless to continue the discussion.

She moved away from him in annoyance.

Kofi, Kwashie's Son, Visits His Father

Kwashie looked at his watched and noticed the time. He then said, "I must pray."

He had built several shrines in which he and the other men (and at special times, women), of the village went to pray to their gods. They sought them for help, strength, protection and a bigger catch of fish.

He remembered he must pray for his son, Kofi, who had been living with one of his brothers; whom he had not seen for a long time.

Just as Kwashie prepared to step backward, as was the custom, into the one-room enclosure which housed some of his gods, his son Kofi approached him.

"Father," Kofi shouted, "I have just received word that I have been accepted at the university." The shock of what Kofi said was a like a physical blow, Kwashie stumbled.

Had Kofi not been quick, Kwashie would have fallen.

Kwashie said, "It is not that I am unhappy to receive your good news. I already have problems. I don't know where I will get the men, I need to continue this village. Now you bring me this news. I have always wanted the best for you, my son. But I had thought the best way for you was to learn to be a fisherman and follow my footsteps."

As Kofi stood looking at his father in disbelief, he heard his father speaking to himself as if delirious.

"What went wrong? Why isn't Kofi interested in fishing?" Suddenly, Kwashie turned to Kofi and questioned, "Haven't I taught you and your young brothers how to mend nets? Haven't you stood and watched me and my men paint the fishing boat? Haven't you and your brothers been here waiting with the other schoolmate boys at the village to welcome me and the other fathers' home from our fishing trip? Haven't you helped me and my men pull in the nets? You always greeted me and the other fathers with enthusiasm as you and your friends beat out those rhythms you boys created."

Kwashie wondered, "Hadn't Kofi listened with the other boys as he and the other fishermen related stories suggesting the excitement of fishing?"

Suddenly in an angered voice, Kwashie said to Kofi, "Why has none of this excitement of fishing rubbed off on you, Kofi, my eldest son? Why have you chosen to be different?"

Kofi knew that this was not the moment to speak. His father's questions, he knew, were not for him. They were questions he supposed every parent might ask of himself at some time.

He kept quiet and watched his father who seemed deep in thought.

Kwashie knew, as did the other parents in the village, there were schools nearby. He, as did the other fathers, encouraged the children to attend school. Since attendance by law had not been compulsory and he was away from home much of the time, most of his sons did as they pleased

At that time, he remembered thinking, "Since the boys will follow my trade, is school necessary?"

Apparently, for Kofi, it had been and it seemed that he was now going to prove its usefulness.

During all this time Kofi had been tenderly holding his father and feeling great compassion for him. While supporting his father, and wiping his brow Kofi said, "Father, I thank you for allowing me to get my basic education"

Kwashie hardly heard Kofi as he remembered the many times while his other sons delighted in learning all they could about fishing, his eldest son seemed far away in thought. While other boys made ropes, played instruments, danced, and sang Kofi, Kwashie recalled, sat quietly with a book.

When did you decide not to become a fisherman, Kofi?" Kwashie demanded abruptly.

"I cannot say, Father, I suppose it was long ago."

"I remember when I was quite young that the zeal of learning did not exist in this village for large numbers of children."

"Learning what," interrupted his father.

"Learning to read, to write," answered Kofi. "While some boys and girls attended school, more did not. In fact," he continued, "many of them who did not attend school couldn't tell you their age."

"Not you, my son. I remember you wanted to know everything. I can still remember the many times you rushed through your chores of fetching water with your three sisters, or swept my room in haste, only to sit down and read your school books."

"Yes, by the time I was twelve, as I recall, I became intensely interested in science. I had noticed that you and the other men chose not to go fishing when the waters were rough. I knew from your account that you told time from the sun and the moon. I was burning with a desire to learn more about the tides, the seasons, the world, the universe."

"You have answered my question son."

For Kofi, there had never been a question. His world had been the village until he discovered another world outside. His world--his village--had been a place where, though it had been said that formal education was important, it was expected that young men would follow their father's tradition. Never mind about the girls, thought Kofi. Their problem is not the same. They would not need a formal education to marry, to bear children, or to be the wives of fishermen.

By the time Kofi had wiped his father's brow, he had finished with his nostalgic thoughts. He was ready to leave. Somehow, he understood his father's reaction. He knew his father would recover. He thought of the sisters and brothers he was leaving behind. They would help his parents forget, he hoped.

Kwashie's California Guests Arrive

After praying, Kwashie stood straight and proud with regained composure.

As he did so, he gave a half smile. He looked up to see a little girl running down the pathway leading into their village. As she ran, she shouted in Eve, the tribal language spoken in Cape Coast, West Africa, "A-fet, Kwashie! Amea-dewa le di wom." When translated the message stated was, "Kwashie, some people are looking for you."

Kwashie patted her head gently as he approached the visitors. Would they, he wondered, want to have him recount his story. Would they want to learn of a poor fisherman's problems? He guessed not as he welcomed his guests with outstretched hands as the villagers gathered round. For this moment he would forget his problems. He was a man of resolution. He would enjoy his guests.

www.ingramcontent.com/pod-product-compliance
Lightning Source LLC
Chambersburg PA
CBHW040753010826
48981CB00032B/316